The Phantom Phunbook

Mark Burgess

MAMMOTH

First published in Great Britain 1991
by Mammoth, an imprint of Mandarin Paperbacks
Michelin House, 81 Fulham Road, London SW3 6RB

Mandarin is an imprint of the Octopus Publishing Group,
a division of Reed International Books Ltd

Copyright © Mark Burgess 1991

ISBN 0 7497 0905 7

A CIP catalogue record for this title
is available from the British Library

Printed in Great Britain
by Cox & Wyman Ltd, Reading, Berkshire

The Phantom Phunbook

Also by Mark Burgess

The Birthday Joke Book
Can't Get to Sleep
Feeling Beastly
Feeling Peckish

Contents

Witches and Wizards

Witches

If you ever meet a witch, watch out. She'll turn
you into a frog as soon as look at you, so hop
it before she gets the chance.

Just so that you know what to look out for, here is a witch and some of her things. You can tell she's not too keen on housework.

Fowl smell

Witch's Hag bag

Coven gloves

Broomstick

Foul Fowl

Cauldron (called Ron)

RON

A Witch's Hat

If you want to look like a witch, it's really quite
easy. You don't need to wash and you don't
need to tidy your room before you start, but
you must have a witch's hat. Otherwise there's
no point. Here's how you can make one:

You'll need two large sheets of paper or thin
card. Use black paper if you can, or paint your
hat black.

Roll one sheet
into a cone.

Tape the end
securely, then trim
the base.

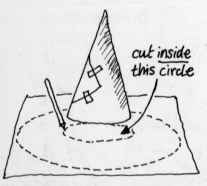

cut inside
this circle

Put the cone on the
second sheet of paper
and draw round it.
Draw a large circle for
the edge of the brim.
Cut round both circles.

slide
brim
down
over
hat

Tape the brim to
the hat and then
paint it. Make a
spider from some
black wool knotted
together.

Warts

Mash up some bread with a little water to make a really sticky dough. (Brown bread looks best.) Roll the dough into tiny balls and it will stick to your face – perfect warts!

Long Fingernails

Cut fingernails from thin card and paint them black or green – then tape them on to your fingers.

curve the card
for a better
fit ➔

Halloween

A witch and her broomstick are seldom parted. It's how she gets around. A quick dollop of flying ointment, then on to the broom and she's off before you can say 'pickled newt'.

At midnight on Halloween, thousands of witches sweep the sky. When it's completely clean, they all land and dance around an enormous bonfire, cackling and laughing, until dawn.

Pumpkin Lantern

A pumpkin lantern is a good way to keep the witches from your door on Halloween. You'll need a large pumpkin and a small torch or candle nightlight (only use the nightlight if the lantern is going outside).

First of all, get a grown-up to help you, as pumpkins are very hard to cut. The top must be sliced off – then you can scoop out the flesh and seeds. Next, draw a face on the pumpkin with a felt-tip and ask the grown-up to help you cut it out (triangles are easier than circles). Then pop the light inside and put the lid on. There, a grinning face in the dark – no trouble from witches tonight!

Witch's Cauldron Game

Witches love playing games. This is one of their favourites.

You'll need a large washing-up bowl or bucket for the cauldron, all sorts of things to put in it, a large black plastic rubbish bag that you can't see through, and some paper and pencils for everybody. (If you're going to have this game at a party, make sure everything is ready beforehand.)

Find about five objects, as different from each other as possible. Here are some ideas: a cold, cooked sausage; a rubber glove (blow it up and tie some string round the wrist to keep the air in); a peeled hard-boiled egg; a hairbrush; a balloon with water in it; a piece of bread squeezed into a lump; a knobbly stick; a used teabag; a peeled grape; some cold, cooked spaghetti; a wet handkerchief.

Urghh, and it's off...

Arrange the objects in the bowl and then tape the open end of the rubbish bag over the top. Make sure it's fixed all the way round. Then cut a hole in the other end of the bag, just large enough for someone to put their arm inside. Now all is ready.

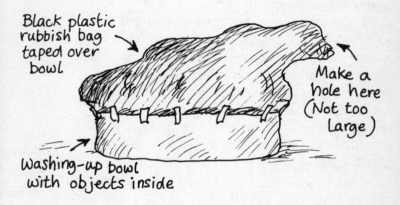

Black plastic rubbish bag taped over bowl

Make a hole here (Not too large)

Washing-up bowl with objects inside

Put the cauldron on a table and make sure everybody has a paper and pencil. Each person in turn has to put their hand through the hole in the plastic bag and then write down what they think is in the cauldron. Read out all the answers at the end and reveal the true contents. The person with the most horrible ideas wins!

Wizards

You should watch out for wizards. They'll turn you into a bat if they get the chance. So if you meet a wizard, don't hang about.

Wandering Wand Game

All you need for this game is a hat (any sort will do), a piece of string, a bottle and a wand (a pencil will do). Tie or tape one end of the string to the hat. Tie the other end round the pencil. Put on the hat. Now try to get the pencil into the bottle without using your hands. See how quickly you can do it!

Wizard's Hat Game

For three or more players
You need to prepare this game beforehand.
You'll need a wizard's hat, which you can
make in the same way as the witch's hat (see
page 10) but without a brim. Now you need
some old magazines. Cut out pictures of
different things and paste them on to the
outside of the hat; about twenty pictures will
do. Hide the hat until you want to play the
game.

Give everyone a pencil and paper and tell
them to stand in a circle. Put on your wizard's
hat and walk about inside the circle for about
three minutes. Make sure everybody has got
a good look at the hat, then take it off and hide
it. Now everyone must write down as many
things as they can remember having seen on
the hat. When everybody's finished writing,
bring out the hat and see who has remembered
the most things. The person with the best
memory wins.

Bob Apple

This ancient game is still played by witches and wizards everywhere. Find a place to play where it doesn't matter if you make a mess, or spread lots of newspaper on the floor. You'll need two bowls of water and some apples.

Choose two teams and a starting line. Place the bowls of water the same distance from each team with an equal number of apples in each bowl. On the word 'Go' the game starts and each player in turn must run to their team's bowl and then grab an apple to bring back – but only using their teeth. The first team to empty their bowl wins.

At last, a game I can get my teeth into.

Cats' Tongues

Witches and wizards love making these little biscuits. They're delicious with squashed fly ice cream but any other ice cream will do just as well.

You need:

    50g (2oz) butter
    50g (2oz) caster sugar
    2 egg whites (get a grown-up to show you how to separate an egg)
    50g (2oz) plain flour

Ask a grown-up to switch the oven on to 220° C (425°F, Gas mark 7).

In a mixing bowl, beat the butter with a wooden spoon for a few minutes until it's soft, then add the caster sugar. Keep beating until the mixture is light and fluffy. (This is rather hard work so if there is a large witch or wizard about, get them to help you.) Gradually beat in the egg whites and then mix in the flour – do this gently so that the mixture stays light and fluffy.

Grease a baking tray with the butter paper and then dust it with a little flour. Now spoon the mixture into a plastic bag and twist the top shut. Holding the bag over the baking tray, cut off a corner with a pair of scissors to make a small hole and then squeeze out the mixture on to the tray. Make finger lengths about 3cm (1 inch) apart as the biscuits will spread out while they're cooking.

Using oven gloves, put the biscuits into the oven and bake them for 4–5 minutes until they are golden and just brown around the edges. Then carefully lift the biscuits off the baking tray with a metal spatula or knife (they'll be very hot) and put them on a wire rack to cool.

What is the witch using to make her spell? Fill in the crossword to see.

The wizard is saying a vegetable spell. What are the vegetables?

Answers on page 96.

Witches

Witches never wash themselves.
They never comb their hair.
They never clean their clothes at all
Or change their underwear.
Their skins are always spotty
(Exactly as you'd guess).
They're dirty and they're mucky,
They always look a mess.
They've lots of creepy crawlies,
Like cockroaches and fleas,
Which crawl about their bodies
And do just as they please.
That's why witches scratch and scratch,
How horribly they itch –
I'm really glad that I am me
And not a warty witch!

One Dark Halloween

Some witches, one dark Halloween,
Cooked up a most horrible scheme
To rob girls and boys
Of all of their toys –
How wicked, how nasty, how mean!

But the children, of course, joined the fun.
Those witches, they caught on the run
And put the whole coven
Straight into an oven.
I'm sure that, by now, they are done.

Witch and Wizard Jokes

Witches like jokes a lot. They enjoy a good cackle, except for when they laugh so much that they fall off their broomsticks. They don't find that so funny.

Wizards like jokes too. Tell a wizard a good joke really slowly and he'll be enchanted.

What's a witch's favourite food?
Coven-ready chicken and chips.

What do old witches suffer from?
Broomatism.

What sort of witch can you eat?
A sandwich.

What did the wizard put on his fish and chips?
Tomato sorcery.

How can you tell if a wizard has a false tooth?
When it comes out in conversation.

What do witches ask for at hotels?
Broom service.

Why did the wizard go to the North Pole?
For a cold spell.

What happens when a witch loses her temper
while riding her broomstick?
She flies off the handle.

What do you call a wizard on a broomstick?
A flying sorceror.

How did the owl feel when the wizard used the
wrong spell on him?
He didn't give a hoot.

Why did the witch give up gazing at her
crystal ball?
There was no future in it.

Where do you send a short-sighted frog?
The hoptician.

Why shouldn't you eat frogs and toads?
You might croak yourself.

What do you get if you cross a skunk with
a witch?
A very bad spell.

What happened when the frog-prince broke
his leg?
He was rushed to hopsital.

What do you call it when witches go shopping?
Haggling.

What do Scottish witches eat on Halloween?
Haggis, of course!

Skeletons

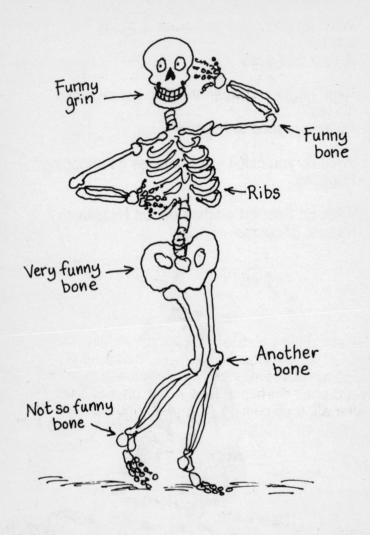

Funny grin →

→ Funny bone

← Ribs

Very funny bone →

← Another bone

Not so funny bone →

Let's face it, skeletons are pretty hairy – I mean scary. Would you like to meet one? I wouldn't. I think if I did, I'd jump out of my skin.

Skeletons are also lazy; bone idle in fact. They just lie about. Occasionally they hang out in cupboards. Have you got a skeleton in your wardrobe? Perhaps you'd better go and see. After all, they come to life after sundown. . .

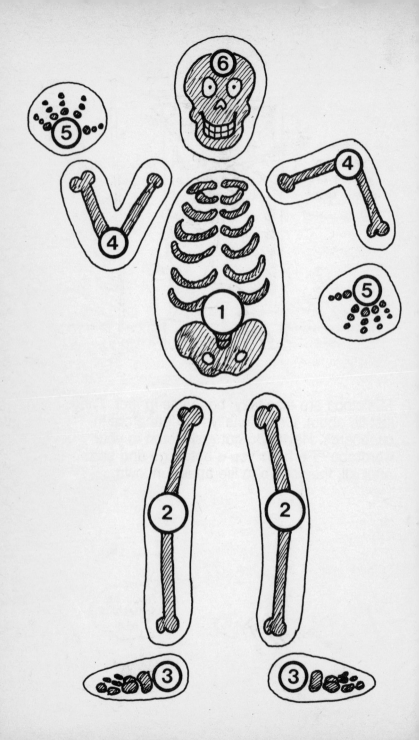

Collect a Skeleton Game

For two or more players
You will need some card in different colours to make the skeletons and a dice to play the game.

   You need to make a whole skeleton for each player. Copy this skeleton on to card. (Make sure you number each piece correctly.) You could use a different colour for each skeleton you make. Cut carefully round all of the pieces.

To play Lay the bones on the floor, jumbled up, but all facing upwards. Each player in turn has a throw of the dice. A 1 is needed to start and then that player can take a body. The other bones are collected as follows: a 2 for each leg, then 3 for each foot and so on until a 6 is thrown for the head. The first person to get a whole skeleton is the winner.

At last,
somebody to
play with...

Skeleton Food

Skeletons live on next to nothing. They just
don't have the stomach for much food. But
here is one of their favourites.

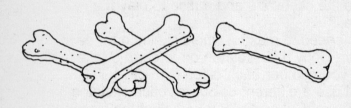

Spookhetti and Ghost

You need several slices of soft white bread
and some spaghetti in tomato sauce. With a
pair of scissors, cut out bone shapes from the
slices of bread. (Don't make them too small.)
Also cut out a ghost or tombstone for each
person. Then put the shapes on a baking
sheet and crisp them in a slow oven. (Ask a
grown-up to turn it on to 160°C [325°F, Gas
mark 3].) Don't let the pieces go too brown –
15 minutes should be long enough.

Serve up the spaghetti with the bones and
a ghost or tombstone planted on top!

Urghh-
worms,
not for me!

Bone-ana Milkshake

Milk is good for the bones. That's why skeletons like drinking it. I've forgotten what bananas are good for. . . Oh yes, the memory.

For this delicious milkshake you'll need:

1 banana (the riper the better)
About a teaspoonful of honey
A pinch of grated nutmeg
250ml or ½ pint of milk
A couple of ice cubes

If your house has a blender, ask a grown-up to whizz all the ingredients together for about a minute. If you don't have a blender, then leave out the ice cubes, mash up the banana with the honey and the nutmeg in a deep bowl and then gradually whisk in the milk. Whisk until it's really frothy! Then the milkshake's ready.

I'll go bananas if I don't have one soon.

Love Story

Two skeletons once fell in love.
Each night was perfect bliss –
They'd dance beneath the moonlit trees,
They'd cuddle and they'd kiss.

But then, alas, they fell apart,
As though it hadn't mattered.
One left – she hadn't any heart –
The other one was shattered.

Here lies the body of
Jovial Jim
People were so fond of him.
He'd tell a joke, he'd make them laugh—
What better for an epitaph?

Alas, poor Jim fell mortal sick
And laughing, died. (The end was quick.)
He's buried now beneath this hill.
But listen; there—
He's laughing still.

The Phantom Bantam

Don't ever stay at Crowsfoot Farm.
You'll hardly sleep at all –
It's haunted by a ghostly fowl
Which walks along the wall.

Each night the Phantom Bantam strides,
On legs a little shaky.
And, crowing ghoulishly, it cries:
'It's night-time – wakey, wakey!'

Wrap Up, Everybody!

The ancient Egyptians had dead people really wrapped up. Loo paper is great for getting wrapped up like a mummy. (Ask a grown-up before you use it.)

You'll probably need more than one roll, especially if more than one person is getting wrapped up. Just wind the paper round and round until your whole body is covered. You might need someone to help. Have a competition to see who can get wrapped up the fastest.

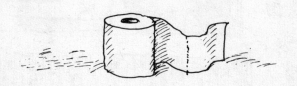

How quickly can you find your way through the graveyard?

Skeleton Jokes

Skeletons like jokes. Especially rib-ticklingly funny ones. And they enjoy parties – skeletons love a rattling good time. But usually they haven't got any body to go with. That makes them sad. So next time you meet a skeleton, cheer it up with a good joke – it'll probably collapse with laughter.

What goes ha, ha, thump, thump, thump, thump, thump?
A skeleton laughing its head off at the top of the stairs.

How do skeletons communicate?
With cryptic messages.

Who manned the phantom ship?
A skeleton crew.

What musical instrument do skeletons play?
Trombones.

What did the skeleton say to his girlfriend?
I love every bone in your body.

What do skeletons eat their food off?
Bone china.

What did one angry skeleton say to the other?
I've got a bone to pick with you.

How do skeletons talk long distance?
By telebone.

Why did the skeleton go to the graveyard?
He wanted to dig out a few friends.

Where's the local cemetery?
At the dead centre of town.

How do you make a baby skeleton happy?
Give it a rattle.

Vampires

Vampire Hat →

Vampire Bat

← Vampire Flats

Vampires are easy to recognize. They are always impeccably dressed and if they should pass you in the street they'll smile pointedly at you. Then you'll know. Some vampires have a really captivating smile. But don't get taken in. They're after one thing and one thing only: *your blood*. Fortunately, vampires are such suckers that if you offer them a blood orange they'll go for that instead, so make sure you keep one handy.

Bats

Bats tend to hang around vampires. But not all bats are vampire bats, so if you see a bat, don't get in a flap.

Garlic

It is a well-known fact that a necklace made from garlic will protect you from vampires. Eat some and everybody else will leave you alone as well.

Beat that, Dracula...

Vampire Fangs

A bit of orange peel makes frightfully good vampire fangs. Cut an orange in quarters, and peel one of the quarters carefully. Now cut the peel like this:

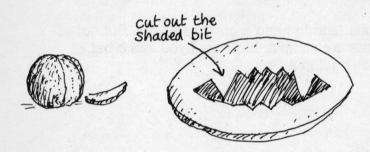

cut out the shaded bit

Pop the piece of peel in your mouth behind your lips. Urghh!

To complete the picture, you could whiten your face with flour. If you dampen your face slightly first, the flour will stick better. For some blood-red dribbles from your mouth, borrow your mum's lipstick or use tomato sauce.

Fangtastic!

Vampire Drinks

If you fancy drinking something which *looks* like blood, try one of the following:

Tomato juice
Ruby grapefruit juice
Blood orange juice
Cranberry juice

Make sure you drink it out of a clear glass so that everyone will see you're drinking blood.

You could add a little bat to the glass. Here's

how. Copy this bat on to black paper or card, then cut it out. You can either stick it to the glass with a loop of sticky tape, or use a paper clip. Open the paper clip out a little, then stick it to the back of the bat with tape. The bat can now be pushed on to the rim of the glass.

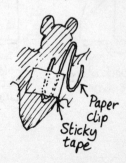

Paper clip
Sticky tape

Bats in the Belfry

Bats like this game; they'll fly in and out of the belfry all night. Here's how you can play.

You'll need a bat dart for each person. Make each dart from a rectangular piece of paper like this:

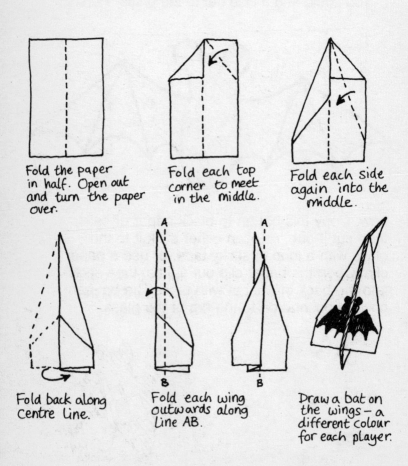

Fold the paper in half. Open out and turn the paper over.

Fold each top corner to meet in the middle.

Fold each side again into the middle.

Fold back along centre line.

Fold each wing outwards along line AB.

Draw a bat on the wings – a different colour for each player.

For the belfry you'll need a large sheet of paper – as large as possible. Newspaper will do, or some unwanted wallpaper. Cut belfry windows in the paper – large ones and small ones, but all large enough for a dart to go through. Use a felt-tip to number each window for scoring, with the smallest window getting the highest score. Tape up the belfry between two chairs.

Draw stones to make it look like a wall.

When all is ready, take it in turns to throw a bat dart at the belfry. After ten goes each, the person with the highest score is the winner.

Really batty.

Count Dracula

One day to Count Dracula's castle
The postman delivered a parcel.
Inside was a note
From his mother, who wrote,
'Come over and see me, you rascal.'

The Count sent a speedy reply
Saying, that very night he would try
To call on his mum
At a quarter to one,
And thanks very much for the tie.

The Count kept his word like a gent
And he took her a bottle of scent.
His mum was delighted
And promptly ignited
The steak which for supper was meant.

They dined and they chatted till dawn
When Dracula said, with a yawn,
'I'll burn like a bun
If exposed to the sun –
So, really, I'd better be gone.'

So he gathered his cloak for the flight
And he promised his mum he would write.
Then he gave her a peck
On the side of the neck
And he took off into the night.

Vampire Jokes

Vampires enjoy a joke. Tell them a good joke about a long neck and they'll be internally grateful. But whatever you do, don't mention wooden stakes or the sun. That'll make their blood boil.

What happens if Dracula knocks you out?
You're out for the Count.

Why does Dracula gargle every morning?
To stop bat breath.

What does Dracula do at a cricket match?
He's the vumpire.

What do you get if you cross a vampire with a yeti?
Frostbite.

Where does Count Dracula keep his armies?
Up his sleevies.

Does Dracula drink coffee?
Only de-coffinated.

What exercise does Dracula like?
Vaulting.

What does Dracula drink out of?
A jugular.

What did the vampire dentist say?
'Necks, please.'

How can you tell when Dracula has a cold?
From his coffin.

What do vampires like for tea?
Clotted scream.

What does Dracula keep in his bat-room cupboard?
His thirst-aid kit.

What do you call it if you find Dracula's coffin?
A grave mistake.

What does an honest vampire do?
Tells the tooth.

What happened to the mad vampire?
He went completely bats.

Can vampires be annoying?
Yes, a real pain in the neck.

Why did Dracula die laughing?
He finally got the point.

Ghosts

Ghosts are really incredible. They have to be seen to be believed. And the things they get up to! There you are, fast asleep in bed and dreaming about summer holidays and chocolate pudding, when all of a sudden there's an icy blast as the sheet is whipped off your bed and somebody says 'Boo!' in your ear. How frightful! That's a ghost all over – always up to every sort of trick. But don't worry, you'll see through most of them. Spooks are so transparent.

Professional ghost hunters have a way of
finding out if it's a real spook they're looking
at, or if somebody is trying to fool them. They
put flour on the floor. Of course, a real ghost
doesn't leave any footprints, so flour will show
up the fakes.

Put flour on your bedroom floor this evening.
You might not see a ghost, but your mother
will go as white as a sheet when she sees it
in the morning.

Favourite Ghost Joke

Headless ghosts haunt large old country houses. They walk about with their heads under their arms. You can pretend to be a headless ghost. All you need is a balloon, a paper bag, some wool, sticky tape, paints or felt-tips and a large overcoat.

Blow up the balloon and tie a knot in it to stop the air escaping. Then put the balloon into the paper bag and tape it together so that it fits the balloon snugly. If you don't have a paper bag you could use pieces of paper to cover the balloon, taping them on one at a time. Paint or draw on your balloon parcel to look like a head and stick on wool for hair. (Don't make it look too pretty or people will say it's an improvement.)

Now you need the large overcoat. Put it on and then lift it up so that you can do up the top button above your head. Do up all the other buttons. Hey presto, you're a headless ghost! Now, where did you put your head. . .

He's always doing that.

A Ghostly Message

When a spook writes a message, there are usually two things to notice: it's written backwards and it's invisible. People don't get many ghost letters, funnily enough. But you can pretend to find one. Here is how you do it.

You need a sheet of paper, a table mat or board, sticky tape, a coloured crayon, a white wax crayon or a white candle, and some watercolour paints. If you write in white wax crayon on white paper then you won't be able to see the message, so that's the invisible bit taken care of.

So how do you write backwards? It's easier than you think. First of all you need to tape the sheet of paper to a table mat or board – hardboard is ideal. You have to be able to press against it while you're writing.

Now turn your board over so that the paper is facing downwards. Hold the board firmly with your left hand (if you're right-handed) and pick up the crayon. It's easier if you're sitting down. Imagine that the piece of board is a sheet of glass and you can 'see' your

Hold board firmly

Imagine you can see your writing through the board as you write.

Write on paper taped to underside

Your writing will be backwards.

message as you write on the paper. Keep your message short! You might need to practise a bit, so use a coloured crayon to start with and check the result in a mirror.

When you've finished writing, show everybody the 'blank' sheet of paper and tell them you think you've found a message from a ghost. How will you make it appear? Simple. You get out your paintbox and slosh watery paint all over the sheet. Strange marks appear . . . but what do they mean? Hold the paper up to a mirror to see!

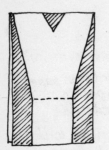  

This whistle makes a noise like the wailing of ghosts in the night. When you blow it, everyone will jump!

You need a strip of greaseproof paper about 20cm × 8cm (8in × 3in). Fold it in half so that the fold comes at the top and then cut away the shaded portions as shown in the drawing. Bend the bottom flaps outwards along the dotted line. Hold the whistle between your forefinger and middle finger and then blow between your fingers.

A Spook For a Pet

Tell your friends you've got a tame ghost. He's so small, he can fit into a matchbox. But there are three matchboxes on the table; which one is he in? You pick up a matchbox and it rattles – so that's where he is!

Mix up the boxes and ask your friends if they can find the ghost. They won't be able to, however hard they try. But *you* can always find the right box.

Here's the secret. You have a fourth matchbox, with small pebbles or a marble inside, tied to your right arm and hidden by your sleeve. The boxes on the table are all empty. If you shake a box with your *left* hand, it will sound empty. But every time you use your *right* hand the matchbox up your sleeve will rattle.

Use bandage or a strip of cloth to secure matchbox

A Spooktacular trick!

Spookie Spuds

These jacket potatoes are just the thing if you've been dancing in the moonlight to haunting melodies.

You need:
A potato for each person
Grated cheese
Sweet pickle or chutney
Butter
Some small pickles or cocktail onions and cocktail sticks

Ask a grown-up to switch the oven on to 190°C (375°F, Gas mark 5).

Give each potato a good wash and scrub so that it's quite clean and then pat it dry with kitchen paper.

Prick each potato with a fork to stop it exploding in the oven. Using oven gloves, put the potatoes into the oven and leave them to cook for about an hour. Mix together about 2 desertspoons of grated cheese and 1 teaspoon of pickle per potato.

When the potatoes are done, take them out (use oven gloves!) and cut a cross in the top of each. If you squeeze gently, the potato will open up – pop a knob of butter inside and then a good spoonful of cheese and pickle on top.

To add the finishing touch, decorate each spooky spud with pickled onions on cocktail sticks – eyes on stalks!

They look like Spooktaters!

What is the ghostly apparition? Join the dots to find out.

Time to go!

The Phantom Coach

One winter's night,
I got a fright
While walking on my own.
I saw approach
A phantom coach –
I wished I was at home.

Each phantom horse
Was black, of course;
Great harness bound their necks.
Their phantom breath,
As cold as death,
Quite misted up my specs.

Then all was clear.
Struck dumb with fear,
I tried, in vain, to hide –
For then, a bloke,
(The coachman) spoke:
'There's room for one inside!'

The Elephant Ghost

The elephant ghost
Of all, is the most
Good-looking and favoured with grace.
He never grows tired
Of being much admired
When haunting his favourite place.

But it's hardly a fluke
That this elegant spook
Is generally thought the most handsome –
For his infinite care
With what he's to wear
Guarantees he's a smart elephantom.

Ghost Jokes

Ghosts love jokes. They'll laugh at nothing.
Tell them a really good joke and they'll
probably shriek with laughter.

What did the doctor say to the sick ghost?
'Sorry, I can't see you now.'

What checks that there's nobody about before
saying 'Boo'?
A very nervous ghost.

Why couldn't the ghost get a drink at the pub?
The barman didn't serve spirits.

What do ghosts do when they retire?
Visit all their old haunts.

What do little ghosts do at Christmas?
Go and see a phantomime.

How do you stop a ghost taking your bicycle?
Put a spook in the wheel.

Which ghost has the best hearing?
The eeriest.

How did the ghosts fall in love?
It was love at first fright.

How do ghosts fly?
In a scareplane.

When does a ghost train stop?
At every manifestation.

When do ghouls go sailing?
When the sea's dead calm.

What do you call a family of ghosts all shrieking at once?
Pretty frightful, relatively spooking.

What do you call ghosts having a Halloween party on top of a mountain?
High spirits.

Where do spooks put their letters?
In a ghost box.

What do you call a ghost who goes round pubs and restaurants, looking in the kitchens?
A public elfin spectre.

Did you hear about the educated ghost?
She went right through school.

73

Werewolves

The werewolf is a cheerful sort,
He's nearly always happy.
He likes to wear outrageous clothes,
His dressing's always snappy.
He'll greet you with a cheery smile,
And ask you in for tea –
But let me tell you straight away,
You'd be foolish to agree.

Howling At the Moon

Werewolves howl at the moon. It's a lot of fun howling at the moon; you should try it. After a bit of practice you'll get quite good at it and probably give the neighbours the shivers. If there isn't a moon then you could use a torch but somehow that's not quite the same.

I used to be a werewolf but I'm not one no-ow-ow-ooowwwww.

Look Your Beast

Werewolves are always well-dressed, so if you want to be taken for one, put on your best clothes. You could make this mask to complete the outfit. You'll need a sheet of thin card, a pencil, a side plate, some felt-tip pens or paints, scissors and some elastic or string.

Copy the mask shape on to the card. Draw round an upturned side plate to get the right size for your face and then add the ears and the nose. Draw in the eyes and mark where the holes for the elastic will be. Colour or paint your mask and then cut it out. Make holes for the elastic by carefully pushing a sharp pencil through the card, then tie on the elastic. Good howling!

Meow - ow
-ow - ooww

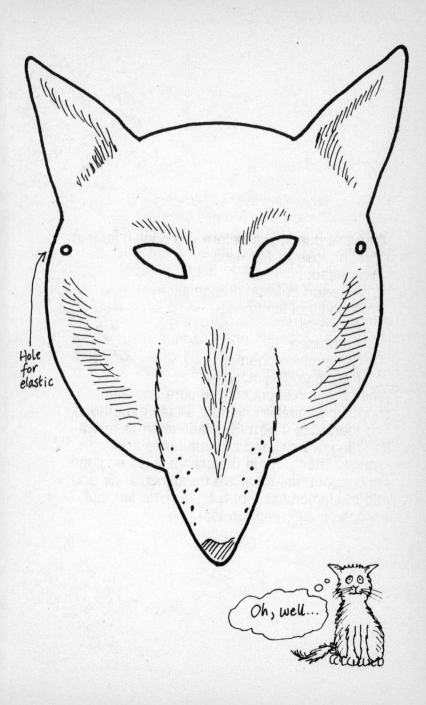

Hole
for
elastic

Oh, well...

Make this punch just before you drink it so that
it doesn't lose its fizziness.

You need:

A carton of fresh orange juice
A bottle of lemonade
An apple
An orange
Some glacé cherries
Ice cream (if you like)

Wash the apple, cut out the core and then
chop it into smallish chunks. Wash the orange
and then slice it. Put the glacé cherries into a
large jug or bowl and add the apple and
orange. Then pour in the orange juice until the
jug is about half-full. Give the punch a stir and
add the lemonade. For a bit of extra fun, put
dollops of ice cream on top!

Wolf Wood

Can you find twenty wolves in the wood?

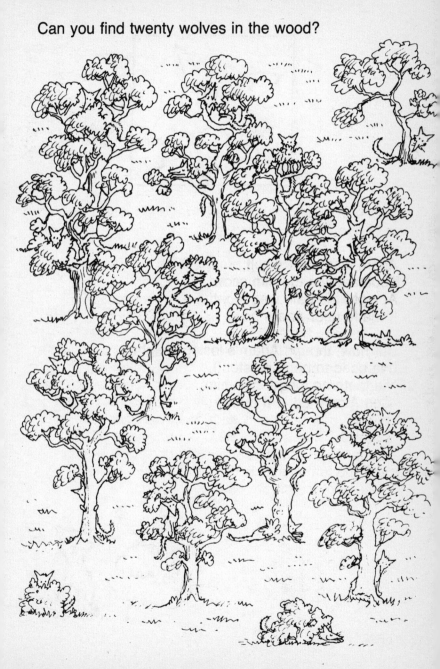

Adam the Werewolf

Adam was a werewolf,
Toothache made him scowl.
At night the pain was frightful –
It made poor Adam howl.

But now, though Adam's losing weight
(He used to be quite stout),
His teeth no longer hurt him
'Cos Adam 'ad 'em out.

By gum!

Werewolf Jokes

Werewolves like a joke. Especially a good one with some nice juicy bits they can really get their teeth into. They particularly like shaggy dog stories. So tell them a shaggy dog story and with a bit of luck they'll forget about what they were going to have for supper. Here's one, just for starters.

It was a dark and stormy night. The wind howled as if there were wolves about the castle. Two travellers struggled up the road, the rain lashing their faces and the wind whipping their cloaks.

At last they reached the castle door. One pulled on the bell-rope and far away, a bell tinkled. It was some time before the door opened. 'Come in,' said a voice, but there was nobody there. The travellers went inside and the door clanged shut behind them.

Inside the castle, there was a fire roaring in the hearth and a wonderful meal was spread out on a table. 'Eat,' said the voice. The travellers were so hungry, they didn't hesitate.

When they had both eaten all they could, the two men drew their chairs closer to the fire. One said to the other, 'Tell us a tale, Bill.' This is the tale he told:

'It was a dark and stormy night. The wind howled as if there were wolves about the castle. Two travellers struggled up the road. . .'

How do werewolves like their shepherd's pie?
With the shepherds nice and tender.

What's the best way to get fur from a werewolf?
Run as fast as possible.

What do you call a man chased by a werewolf?
Claude Bottom.

Monsters

I'm told that the best way to avoid being caught by a monster is to wear your shoes in bed. This makes you completely invisible to monsters. I've done it all my life and I'm still here, so that proves it works. On the other hand – or rather, foot – if a monster *should* catch sight of you, you'll be all ready to run for it.

Another thing you could do is pretend to be a little monster yourself. That way the monster will either be scared silly and run off the moment he sees you, or he will think you're a long-lost cousin and give you a big kiss. As that could be embarrassing, pretend to be a *red* monster right from the start.

They didn't have my size!

The Largest Monster

Mrs Phibber and her monster

The largest monster that ever lived was kept as a pet by Mrs Phibber of Plimsoll-on-Sea. It ate nothing but the glue from the backs of postage stamps. At least, that's Mrs Phibber's story and she's sticking to it.

This monster escaped some time ago. Because of the continuing disappearance of great quantities of postage stamps, it is thought that the monster is still living in a deep, dark cave on Wildmoor. The Post Office are looking into it.

The Great Escape

A hideous monster has caught you. He's saving you for pudding on Friday, so he's locked you in the dungeon. But he's left the key in the lock on the other side of the door, so you can escape. Here's how you do it.

Fortunately you've brought a newspaper with you. You open this out and push it under the door. Then you pick up a straw from the floor (there are straws all over the floor – the monster had a drinks party before you arrived). You push the key back out of the lock with the straw and it drops on to the newspaper on the other side of the door. You then pull the newspaper, with the key on it, back under the door into the dungeon. Now you can unlock the door from the inside and escape. Clever, isn't it?

Watch Your Arm Grow

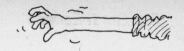

Have you ever wanted to grow really fast? Here's a way to make it look as though you are. Tell your friends you've been kissed by a monster and a weird change is about to come over you. Your arm will grow in seconds.

You need to wear a long-sleeved pullover or jacket. Get your friends to gather round and then stretch out your right arm, but keep it down a little, so that your elbow is close to your body. Now grab your pullover sleeve just below the elbow from behind with your left hand, reaching across your back. Gradually pull the sleeve up towards your armpit. Your friends will be looking at your right hand and shouldn't notice you doing this. It will look just as if your right arm is growing!

I knew you'd be impressed!

Monster Tennis

All you need for this game is a longish piece of string, two chairs, a balloon, and somebody to play with. If there are several people who want to play, then you can split into two teams.

Tie the piece of string between the two chairs so that it is about waist height and fairly taut. Decide who is going to start play. They must throw the balloon into the air and then hit it with their hands *clasped together*. This is the only way you are allowed to hit the balloon and you mustn't unclasp your hands while the game is going on. The object is to hit the balloon *under* the string to the other side. You can hit the balloon as many times as you like, but it mustn't touch the ground on your side of the string. If it does, that's a point to the other side. And you get a point if the other side let the balloon touch the ground.

After each point, take it in turns to start playing again. The first side to 20 points wins the match!

Monster Snaps

Which monster is the odd one out? Give them
all names.

Monster Sale

There's a Monster Sale on in town
At the local all-night store.
There's every sort of monster there,
They're bursting through the door.

The prices are the cheapest yet,
So hurry, don't delay –
It is such fun, the monsters there
Will carry you away.

Monster Jokes

Monsters are fond of jokes. Especially big
jokes that they can really get to grips with.
They've got broad tastes and like jokes about
almost anything, but watch out – if you tell
them a really funny one it could bring the
house down.

Where's the best place to talk to a monster?
As far away as possible.

Which monster had her bicycle stolen?
The Lockless Monster.

What happened to the monster who ran away
with the circus?
The police made him bring it back.

What do you call a monster with a big nose?
E. C. Pickings.

Did you hear about the monster who robbed a
blood bank?
Police are looking for the clot.

What do you call a monster that lives in a
bathroom?
Lucretia.

What do demons eat for breakfast?
Dreaded wheat.

Why did the demon go to hospital?
To have his ghoul stones removed.

Why did the monster go to the restaurant?
Because it was only ten pounds a head.

What does a demon do when he loses his tail?
He goes to a retailer.

Where can you see a monster snail?
At the end of a monster's finger.

Why couldn't the monster finish his sandwich?
His heart wasn't in it.

Answers

Cauldron Crossword, p. 22
1 *across*, thumb; 3 *across*, goo;
6 *across*, eel; 7 *across*, carrot;
8 *across*, bat; 9 *across*, log;
1 *down*, tomato; 2 *down*, beetle;
4 *down*, slug; 5 *down and* 10 *across*,
frog's tongue.

Wizard's Vegetable Spell, p. 23
Parsnip, carrot, lettuce, pea, cabbage.